The Lady with the Alligator Purse

Adapted and illustrated by
Nadine Bernard Westcott

A TRUMPET CLUB SPECIAL EDITION

For
Jim and Sandy
Love, Deanie

ISBN 0-590-98037-8

Published by Scholastic Inc.,
555 Broadway, New York, NY 10012,
by arrangement with Joy Street / Little, Brown and Company (Inc.). TRUMPET and the TRUMPET logo are registered trademarks of Scholastic Inc.

12 11 10 9 8 7   *8 9/9 0 1/0*

Printed in the U.S.A.

Miss Lucy had a baby,
His name was Tiny Tim,

She put him in the bathtub
To see if he could swim.

He drank up all the water,
He ate up all the soap,

He tried to eat the bathtub,
But it wouldn't go down his throat.

Miss Lucy called the doctor,

Miss Lucy called the nurse,

Miss Lucy called the lady
With the alligator purse.

In came the doctor,
In came the nurse,
In came the lady
With the alligator purse.

"Mumps," said the doctor,

"Measles," said the nurse,

"Nonsense!" said the lady
With the alligator purse.

"Penicillin," said the doctor,

"Castor oil," said the nurse,

"Pizza!" said the lady
With the alligator purse.

Out went the doctor,
Out went the nurse,

Out went the lady
With the alligator purse.